THE VERY FIRST EASTER BRUNCH

BY RUBY LYNN PETERSON

A Bubbie & Buddy Book

ISBN 978-1-7348163-0-3

Popover Press LLC Washington, USA

Oh nooooo!

Bubbie does **NOT** know **WHY** we celebrate Easter!

I must help my friend!

I will **get** the Bible, Buddy!

I will **read** the Bible!

THEN...

PARTIES?

We like
parties, too!

At one PARTY, Jesus fed over 5,000 PEOPLE!

The Bible says
mean people killed Jesus!

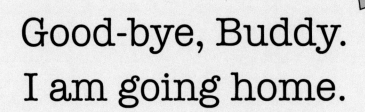

The Bible says **EVIL GUARDS...**

Sealed a **HUGE STONE**
in front of the tomb
where Jesus was laid.
BUT...

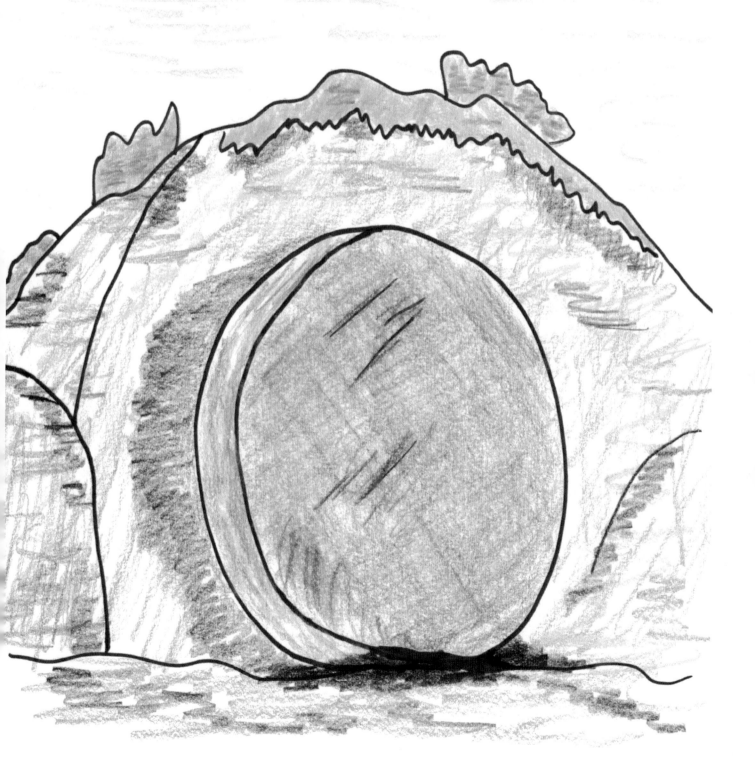

Three

DAYS
LATER

A BIG SHINY ANGEL

WHAM!

THE EVIL GUARDS
FAINTED!

The BIG shiny ANGEL said, "JESUS IS NOT HERE!"

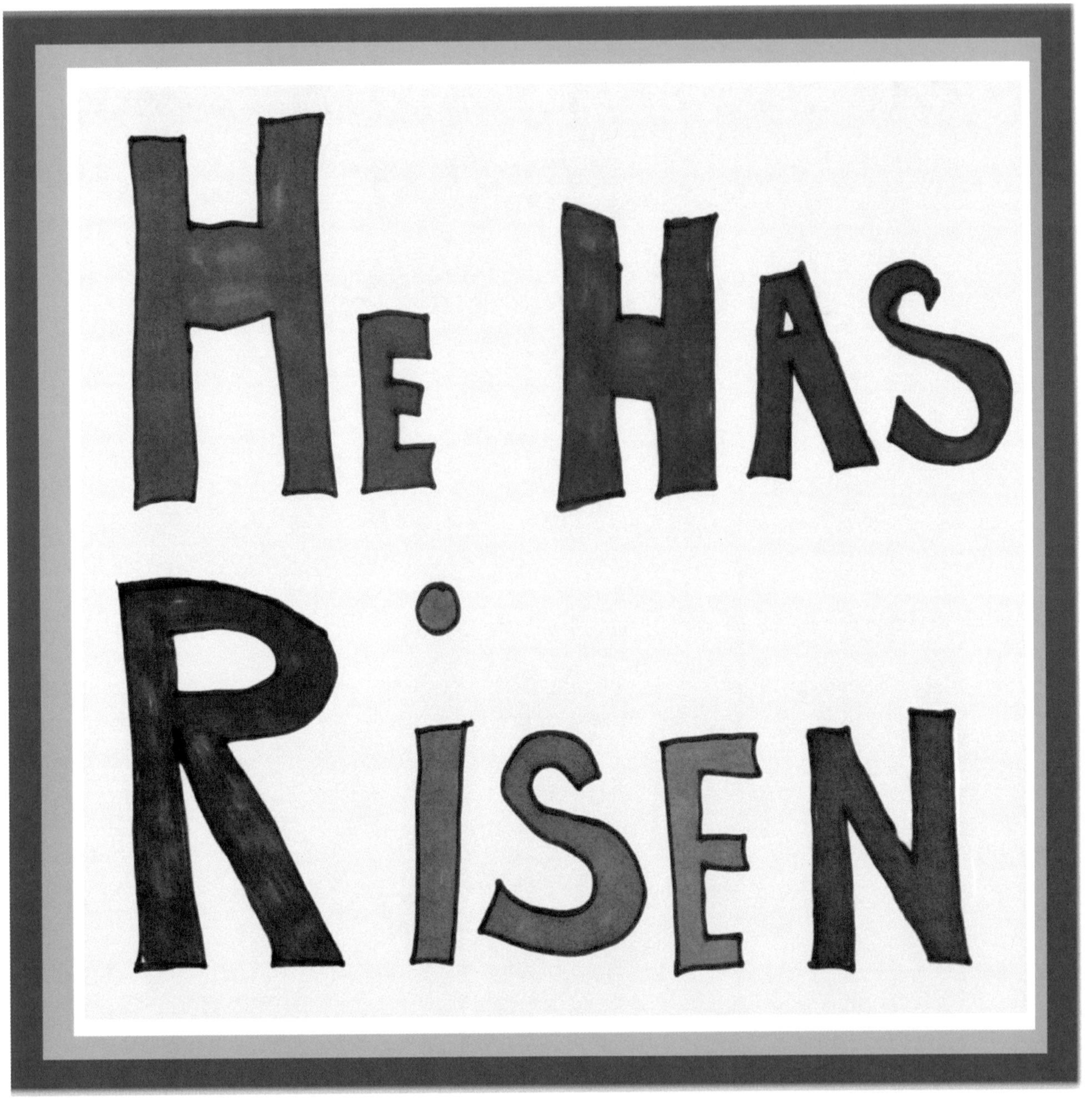
HE HAS
RISEN

HE HAS
RISEN
INDEED!

The Bible says
after Jesus came alive,
He went to the beach...

And made **ROASTED FISH** and **FRESH BREAD...**

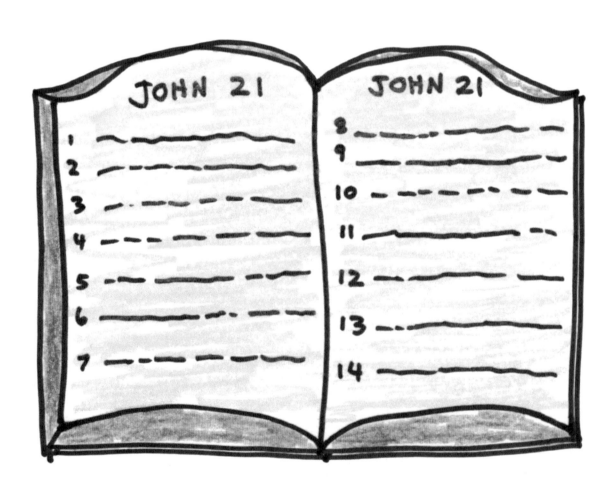

Oh, Buddy!
Jesus made the very first
Easter Brunch because...

The Bible says:

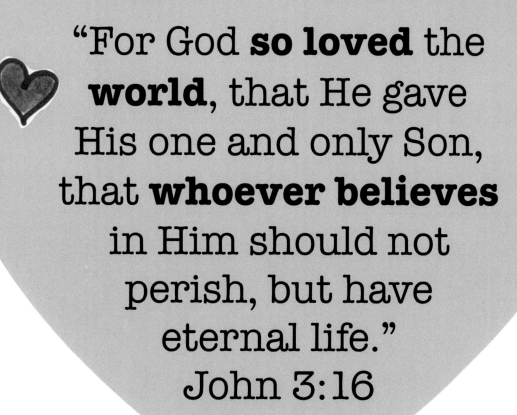

"For God **so loved** the **world**, that He gave His one and only Son, that **whoever believes** in Him should not perish, but have eternal life."
John 3:16

So... LET'S CELEBRATE!

We just love...

EASTER BRUNCH!

Made in the USA
Monee, IL
17 October 2020